LITTLE STORIES

FOR

LITTLE PEOPLE

By

JEANNETTE HALEY

Hidden Manna Publications

LITTLE STORIES
FOR
LITTLE PEOPLE

ISBN: 978-0-9915261-6-1

Cover artwork © Jeannette Haley

Illustrations by Jeannette Haley

The painting of Jesus and the children on the front cover is part of 14 murals painted by the author depicting the life of Jesus that are displayed at the Chapel of the Resurrection in Bothell, Washington

Unless otherwise indicated, Bible quotations are taken from the King James Version of the Bible.

Hidden Manna Publications
www.gentleshepherd.com

CONTENTS

OSCAR'S SECRET

Way down under the ocean lived a clam named Carl. Carl was a happy clam and enjoyed his special spot on the ocean floor.

Carl had a very strange neighbor though. At least Carl thought he was strange because this neighbor didn't seem to be very friendly. His name was Oscar and Oscar was a big oyster.

Carl usually minded his own business.

But one day after weeks of living alone, he

decided to find out why Oscar was so quiet. Slowly, v-e-r-y slowly, Carl opened his shell just a crack so he could get a good look at Oscar.

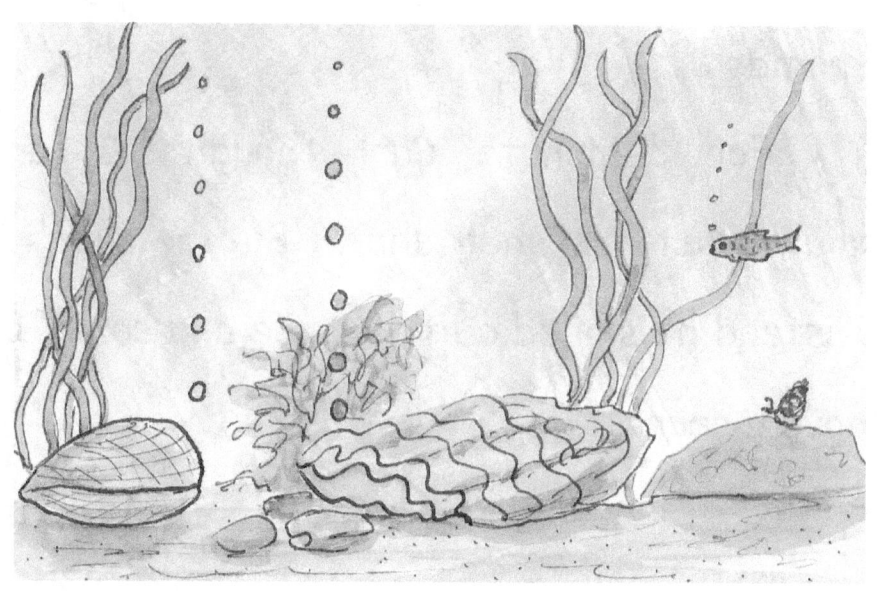

Oscar seemed to be thinking about himself and did not notice Carl. But Carl wasn't going to give up. So he waited and watched, and watched and waited.

After a very long time Carl saw Oscar's shell begin to move. Carl wanted so much to say something, but he kept waiting until Oscar finally noticed him. Then Carl said, "Hello Oscar! I want to be friends."

For a minute Carl thought Oscar might slam his shell shut. But he didn't. Instead he smiled a little smile and said, "I have a secret."

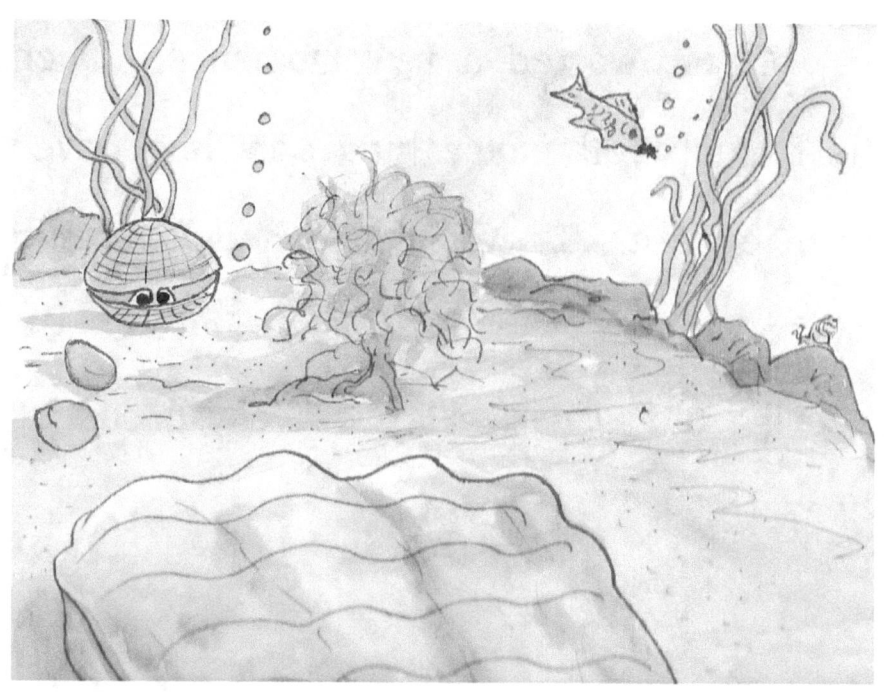

That's strange, thought Carl. *What kind of a secret could an oyster possibly have?* More than anything Carl wanted to know what Oscar's secret was.

"Aren't you going to ask me what my secret is?" asked Oscar.

"Well, yes," answered Carl, "What is your secret?"

Oscar waited a few moments. Then he brought out something Carl had never seen before. It was round and hard and white. It was beautiful! "This is MY pearl!" said Oscar. He was very proud of himself.

Carl wished he had something as wonderful to show Oscar, but he didn't. In fact, he didn't quite know what to say.

Finally, Oscar said, "I suppose I can share my pearl with you, Carl, and then we BOTH will have a secret!" Carl just couldn't believe Oscar said that.

"Wait a minute," Carl replied. "Why have you waited so long to share your wonderful secret with me?"

Oscar was quiet for a long time. Finally, he said, "Carl, to tell you the truth, I am supposed to share this pearl with everyone. But I've been very selfish, and have kept it to myself."

Carl could see that Oscar was truly sorry for what he had done. It wasn't exactly like Oscar had done anything wrong, but he hadn't done anything right either.

"Then we'll have to share this beautiful pearl with others," Carl said. Oscar began to look happier than Carl had ever seen him.

"Yes! That's exactly what we must do!" shouted Oscar.

And so from that day on Carl and Oscar shared their secret with everyone they saw. Now Carl not only was no longer alone, but both he and Oscar were happy because they learned this real secret—and that is, when we share with others what God has given to us, we become more like Jesus. And that makes both our Heavenly Father and us happy! And when we have Jesus in our hearts, we must share Him with others and not be like Oscar who wanted to keep his secret all to himself.

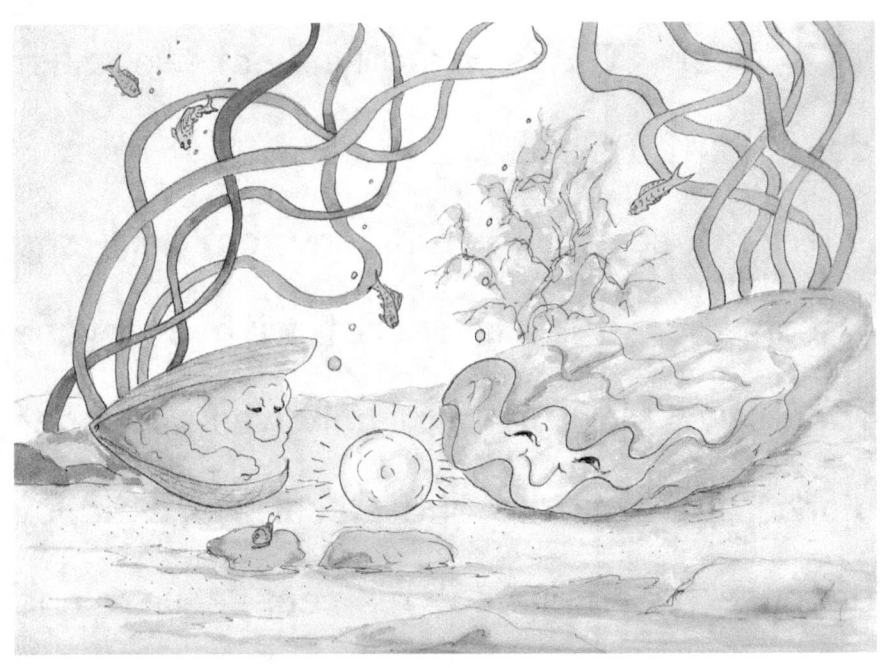

THE LITTLE RED SPARROW

This is the story about a wee little sparrow who lived in some big, tall trees that grew by an old farm house. These trees had lots of leaves in the summer. All the different birds loved to build their nests up in the top branches. They would hop from branch to branch, and sing happy birdie songs.

Now, this wee little sparrow was different from all the other sparrows.

That is because all the other sparrows had brown or gray feathers. But, this little bird had red feathers on his head and breast. So, can you guess what his name was? His name was Red!

Red spent most of his time all by himself. The other sparrows made fun of him because he wasn't the same color they were. He wanted so very much to have at least one good friend to play with. But, the other birds just ignored Red.

Sometimes, he tried to follow the other sparrows when they flew off to find bugs to eat, or water to drink. He felt very sad when they left him behind. So he would fly alone back to his little shady spot hidden beneath the leaves of his favorite tree. At least my mother and father love me, he thought to himself.

Every morning when the sun came up all the birds began singing their favorite bird songs. One morning, wee little Red joined in, and sang his best birdie song.

Suddenly it grew very quiet, and Red noticed that all the other sparrows had flown away. His heart became even lonelier.

This went on day after day until one day something happened that changed everything. Red decided to fly away from the only home he had ever known. He planned to fly as far as he could, and never come back. So, just before the sun came up, he stretched one wing and one leg. Then he stretched the other wing and his other leg. He had to be ready for his long journey.

Quietly, oh! Ever so quietly, Red hopped from branch to branch, going down from the top of the tree. When he knew that the big green leaves hid him from the sleeping sparrows, he quickly flapped his wings and darted out of the tree. He was on his way. He didn't know exactly where he was going, but he hoped it would be a good place where other sparrows would accept him just the way he was.

He hadn't flown very far, though, when suddenly something on the ground caught his eye. What is that? He asked himself. Curiosity got the best of him, so he decided to drop down for a better look.

He landed on the top of a tall, thin black pole-like thing in a beautiful garden full of pretty flowers. Red cocked his head to the left. Then he cocked his head to the right. Then he looked straight down at the wood thing hanging from the black metal pole. *I must be dreaming!* Red chirped softly to himself. *This is so wonderful it has to be too good to be true!* His heart beat faster as he looked at a great big bunch of bird seed.

It was just hanging there, waiting for little birds like him to gobble up the seeds. His tiny feet gripped the smooth wood perch, and he began to eat the delicious seeds.

Red flew to a branch on the flowering butterfly bush next to the bird feeder. *Wow! What is THAT sparkling in the sunshine over there?* Red was getting very excited. *It looks like an itty bitty pond!* (Can you guess what Red had found?) Red had never seen a birdbath before. *Oh! This is such an awesome place!* Red thought joyfully. *I have found the perfect spot for a wee little bird to live. And, it's ALL MINE! ALL MINE!*

Red ate and ate, and drank and drank. Later that day, after the sun had warmed the water in the birdbath, Red hopped in and took a nice, long bath. Finally, he sat on a nearby branch and thought about this heavenly place. It was all a little bird could ask for, except he was still lonely.

Once again Red began to feel very sad. Maybe he should just keep flying until he found some sparrows that looked like him. But, deep inside his heart he knew what the right thing to do was. He still had time if he hurried. So, off he flew, back to the big old trees where his home had been.

All the little brown sparrows stopped flitting about and stared at Red as he flew up into the tree. What was he trying to tell them? There was bird seed? And a birdbath? Red was so excited, he could hardly chirp out the good news. "Follow me, and I'll show you!" he called out, and off he went. "Well, maybe he did find something wonderful," the other sparrows said. "Let's follow him and see for ourselves!" With Red leading the way, they all flew behind him.

Can you guess what happened then? Red became a hero! All the other birds wanted to be his friend. They included him in their games. And, whenever they got together to sing birdie songs, they asked Red to sing along. So, ever after Red was loved and accepted as a very special bird indeed.

BOYS AND GIRLS: Just like Red, who decided to share what he had found, do you know that if you have Jesus Christ in your heart that YOU have something wonderful to share with others? When you tell people about Jesus, you are sharing the BEST news in the whole world with them. Just as Red found food and water for everyone, Jesus is offering spiritual food and eternal water to everyone. And, just as Red found a paradise on earth for little birds, Jesus is in heaven preparing a very special and beautiful place for every one who believes He is the Son of God, and that He came to earth to die for our sins. All we have to do is ask Him to be our Lord and Savior, and receive His gift of eternal life!

THE LITTLE GREEN FROG IN THE SHOE

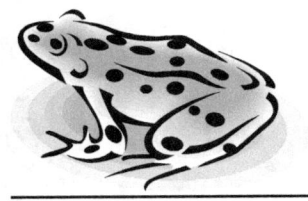

This is a story about Finbar, a very little, and very bright green frog. Finbar in Irish means handsome. Of course little Finbar thought he was the best looking frog around. Because he was so green, he figured he must be Irish too. But, Finbar didn't live in Ireland. Instead, he lived in Nampa, Idaho.

Finbar began his wee life in a small water canal that was filled with all sorts of creatures. There were other frogs, toads, insects, bugs and birds. There were bushes and brambles. But, there were no people because the sides of the canal were very steep and covered with prickly weeds.

Finbar thought he lived in the most wonderful place a frog could live. Then, one day, he saw something that made him change his mind. As he sat quietly watching a bug he thought would make a good dinner, he saw something move in the tall grass beside him. Closer and closer it came towards him. Finbar became frightened. What was this long, skinny thing after, anyway?

Finbar wanted so much to snatch up that bug, but he decided he better pay attention to what was sneaking up on him. Closer and closer it came. Finbar could see its eyes fastened on him, while its tongue darted in and out.

Suddenly Finbar knew what this awful creature was after. It was after him! Finbar's strong back legs sprang into action and he jumped clear across the little canal to the other side. But, he didn't stop there. No siree! He just kept hopping and hopping. He hopped through the prickly weeds and through the bushes until he reached the top of the hill.

Finbar was breathing hard, so he stopped to rest. Everything looked strangely different. He looked behind him and could barely see the little canal through all the grass and bushes. Then he looked in front of him and saw a wonderful sight.

What do you think Finbar saw? Well, he saw all kinds of flowers. They were red and yellow, pink and white. Some were purple and some were orange. Finbar hopped closer to get a better look. He liked what he saw. There were big trees, and right in the middle of it all was the greenest grass he had ever seen.

Right then and there Finbar made up his mind that this would be his new home. After all, bugs are everywhere. He would just hop into this wonderful new world and find a good hiding place.

Finbar found what he thought was the perfect hiding place. He stayed in it during the day when the sun shone bright. Then at night he hopped out so he could sing froggie songs to the night, and catch bugs.

After a few days, when Finbar was sleeping in his special place, his world began to shake. Terrified, he hung on tight and waited to see what was going to happen. Suddenly, a great big thing tried to shove its way into his hiding place! Finbar squealed as loudly as he could. It must have worked, because the thing disappeared. But, then his hiding place got dumped upside down and out he fell.

"What is this cute little frog doing in my gardening shoe?" The lady laughed. Finbar blinked. He had never heard or seen a human before. Maybe I best hop under a flower, real quick, he thought.

Finbar was very upset. That shoe was the best hiding place he had ever had. Maybe he should wait until the human lady put the shoe back on the patio. Then he could sneak in again, and make it his own special place.

And, do you know what? That is exactly what Finbar did! The problem is, a week later he found himself dumped out of his new home again. This is a sad world, Finbar thought. What am I going to do now? I can't go back to that old swampy place where the creepy thing creeps.

Finbar got an idea. He would hop up into a tree so he could get a good view of the yard. This is wonderful, he thought as he hopped onto a branch. I can see everything! Now I can find a good place to live. He looked and looked. Then, he saw it and he begin to sing in his best froggie voice: I see it! I see it! My new home over there! Under the garden shed by the flowers so fair! Finbar was so excited he could hardly wait to hop down.

Now Finbar lives in his own special place. There are bugs everywhere so he always has plenty to eat. No human toes come near his hiding place either. And, in his froggie heart, he sings: The world is a wonderful place for little green frogs.

BOYS & GIRLS: We can learn some lessons from Finbar. He thought everything was fine, and he tried to ignore what was going on around him until the snake almost got him. That is how the devil works. We have to be on guard against the bad things that he wants us to do.

***

But, Finbar was smart, and he left that place in a hurry. When we run away from the devil, God will help us, and save us.

Then Finbar decided he made a good decision to move into a shoe, but he really hadn't. We can learn from this is that before we make a decision, we need to pray and ask the Lord about it.

When the little green frog climbed up into a tree to get a better view of everything, he began to have a whole new way of seeing things from a higher perspective. (Explain perspective.) That is how God wants us to be. He wants us to see things the way He sees them. That way we can make wise choices instead of making foolish decisions and mistakes.

Finally, Finbar found a safe and happy place. The Lord Jesus is in Heaven preparing a place for all those who love Him so that we can be with Him forever.